# Pumpkin Jack

## WRITTEN AND ILLUSTRATED BY WILL HUBBELL

Albert Whitman & Company
Chicago, Illinois

**W**hen Tim carved his first pumpkin, it was fierce and funny and just perfect. A jack-o'-lantern this good deserved a name, so Tim gave it one — "Jack."

**L**ong after the best trick-or-treat candy was eaten,
Tim still kept Jack. At night, when a candle
made Jack's face dance on the wall and filled the dark with
warm pumpkin smells, Tim felt Jack was almost magic.
Yet, too soon, the spell was broken.

**T**his pumpkin is beginning to rot," announced Mom. "It's time to throw it out."

Tim knew it was useless to argue. He carried Jack to the garden, which was filled with the brown ghosts of last summer's plants. "A dead garden is better than a trash can," thought Tim. Still, it made him sad to leave Jack outside and alone.

**W**henever chores or play brought Tim to the garden, he looked at Jack. Every time, Jack was different. He became wrinkled, and his fierce smile began to look silly.

**M**old spread over Jack's bright orange skin. As the days turned colder, Jack grew flatter.

**W**inter began. Soon Jack was hidden beneath snow, and Tim forgot about him.

The cold, heavy-jacket days came. Snowman and sliding days. Indoor days. Thanksgiving, Christmas, and Valentine's. When all these days had passed and the March winds melted the snow, Tim found Jack.

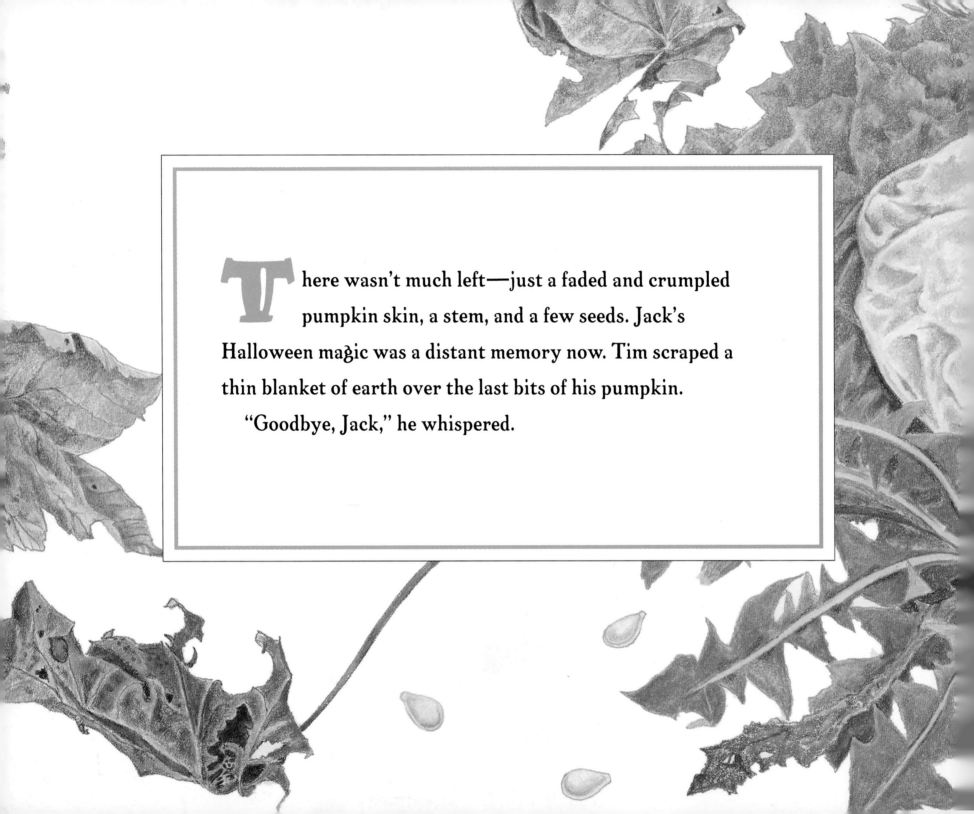

There wasn't much left—just a faded and crumpled pumpkin skin, a stem, and a few seeds. Jack's Halloween magic was a distant memory now. Tim scraped a thin blanket of earth over the last bits of his pumpkin.

"Goodbye, Jack," he whispered.

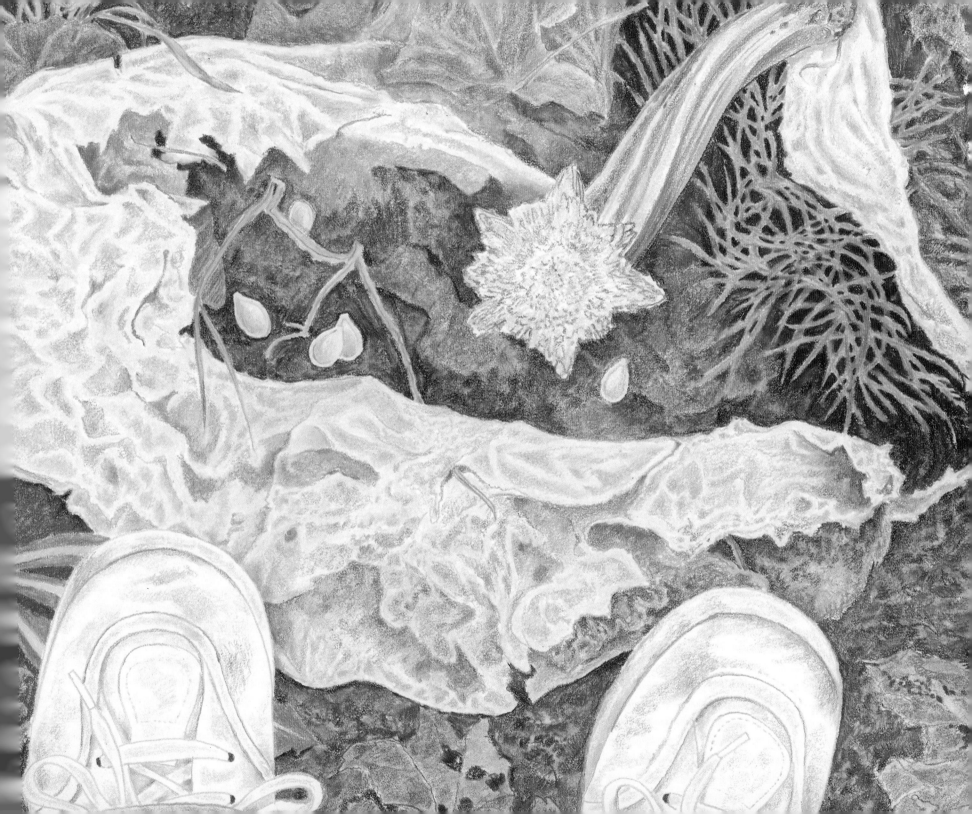

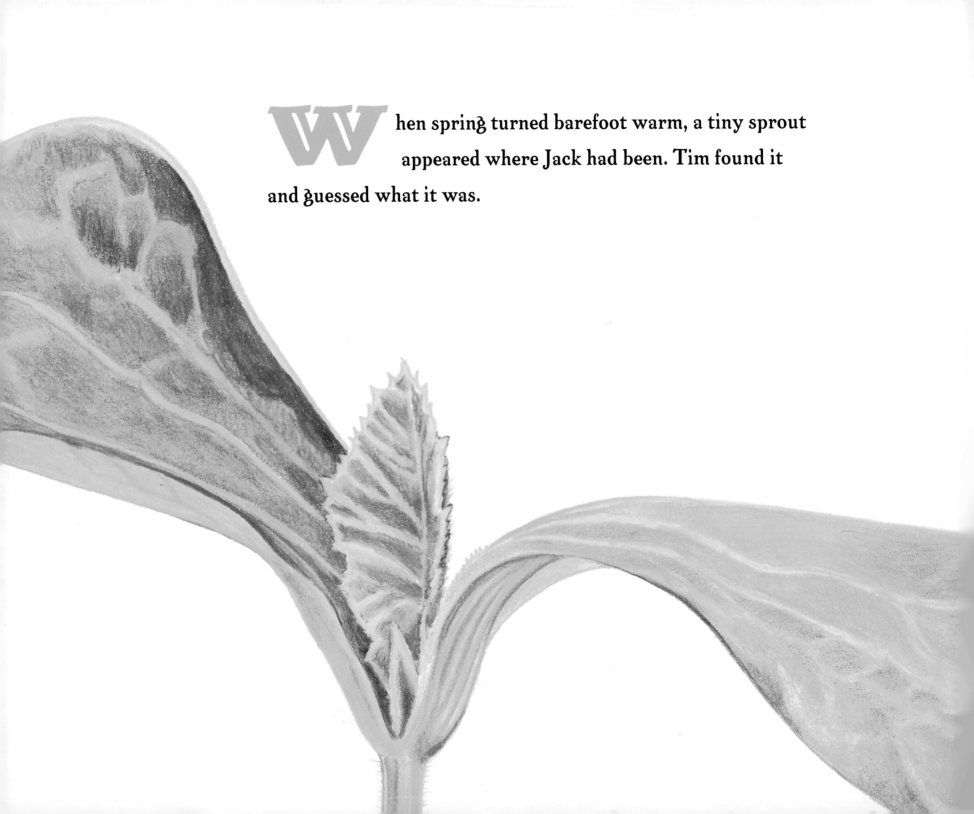

When spring turned barefoot warm, a tiny sprout appeared where Jack had been. Tim found it and guessed what it was.

In the days that followed, Tim weeded and watered and watched the sprout. Slowly and steadily, the plant changed and grew. It branched and spread a web of vines over the ground, but no pumpkins appeared.

The days turned hot. Flowers opened on the plant each morning, yellow stars that twisted shut forever in the afternoon. Still, there were no pumpkins.

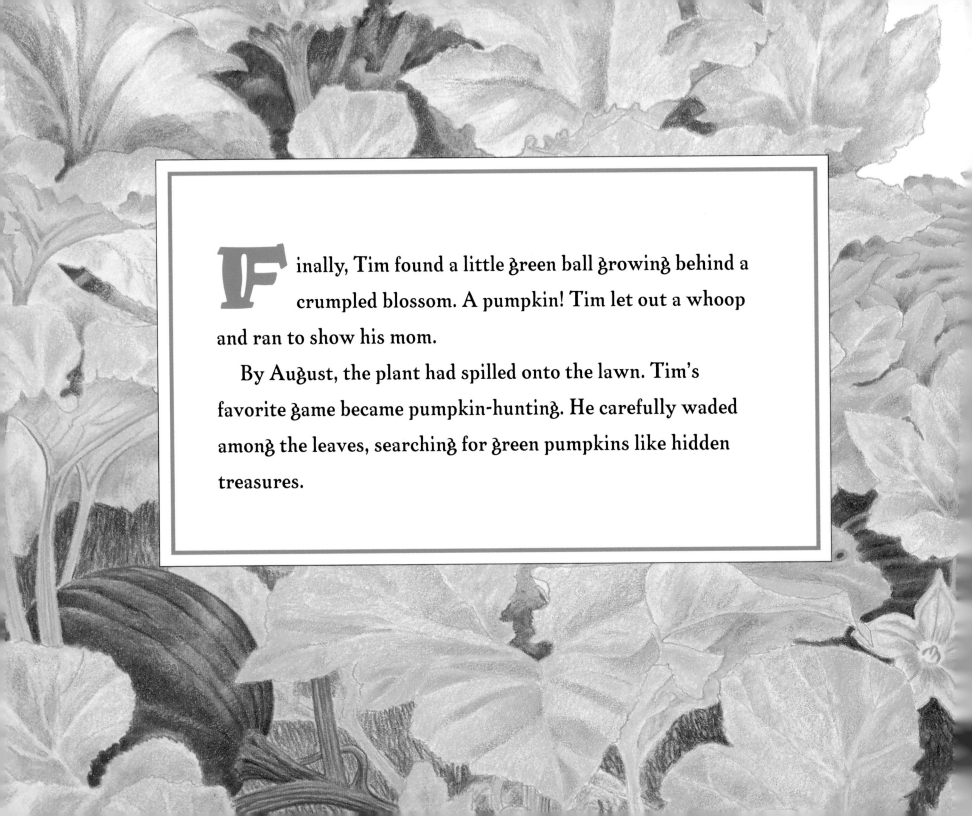

Finally, Tim found a little green ball growing behind a crumpled blossom. A pumpkin! Tim let out a whoop and ran to show his mom.

By August, the plant had spilled onto the lawn. Tim's favorite game became pumpkin-hunting. He carefully waded among the leaves, searching for green pumpkins like hidden treasures.

School began again and the days cooled. Tim had less time to visit the garden. When he did, the pumpkin plant seemed tired. There were few new leaves, and the old tattered ones no longer hid the fat green pumpkins.

Then, one October morning, Tim woke to see frost coating the garden. The frozen plants seemed changed to pale blue glass.

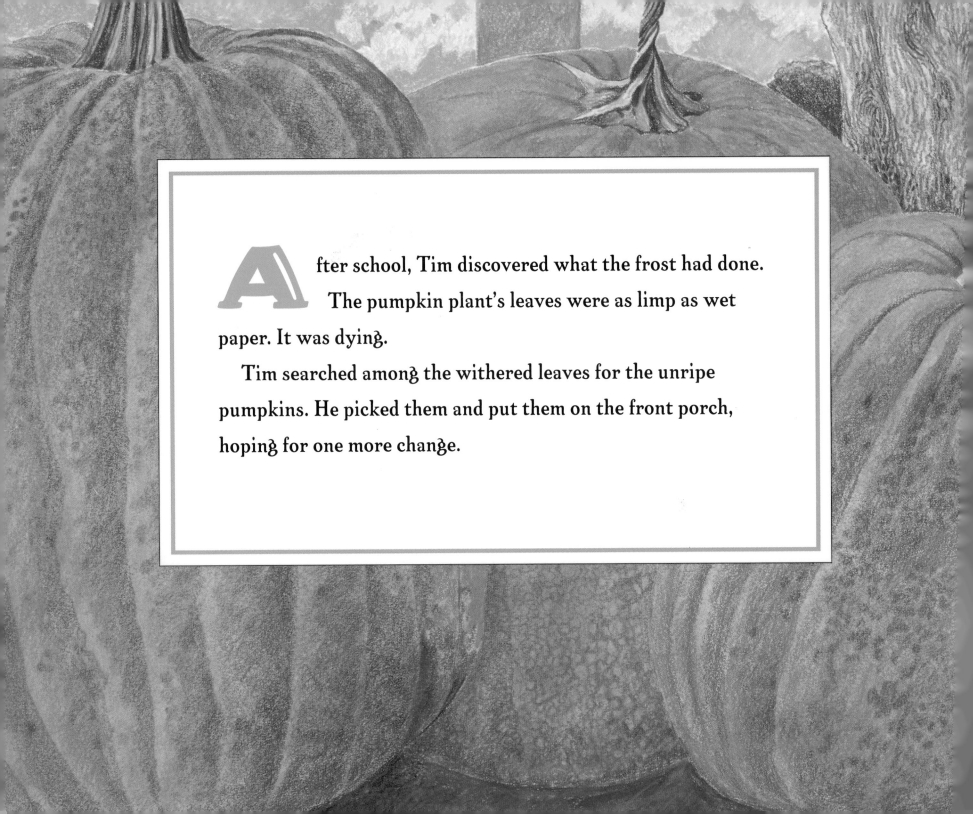

After school, Tim discovered what the frost had done. The pumpkin plant's leaves were as limp as wet paper. It was dying.

Tim searched among the withered leaves for the unripe pumpkins. He picked them and put them on the front porch, hoping for one more change.

By Halloween, the pumpkins had ripened to bright orange. There were many, for the plant had been generous. Tim was generous, too. He gave away all but one.

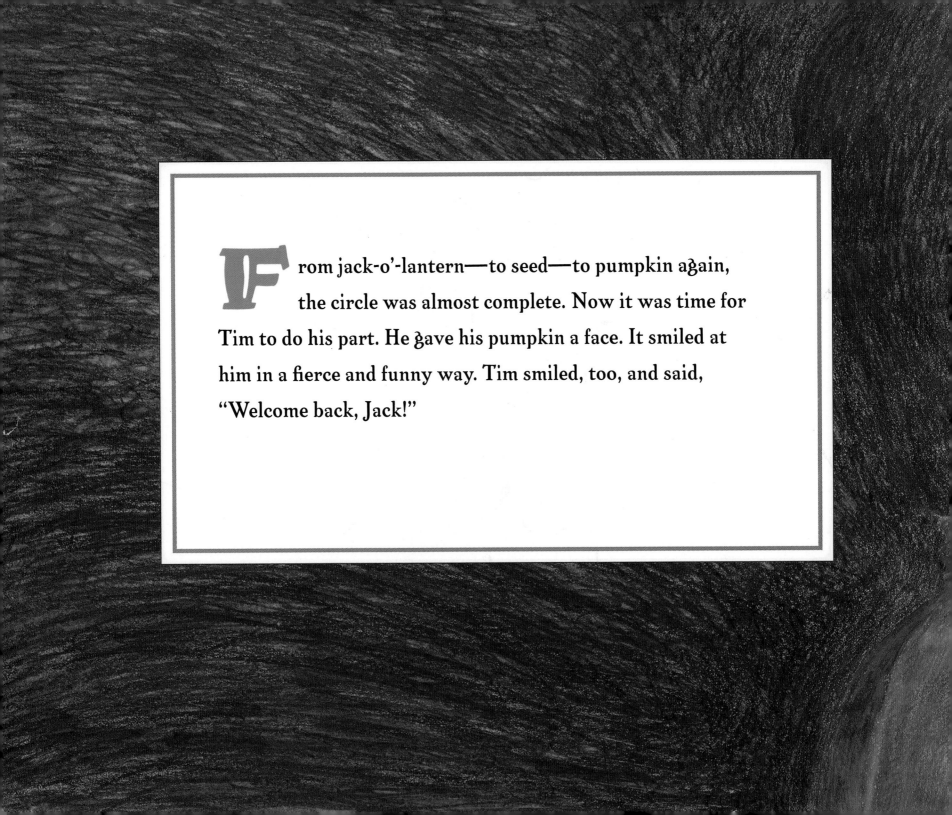

From jack-o'-lantern—to seed—to pumpkin again, the circle was almost complete. Now it was time for Tim to do his part. He gave his pumpkin a face. It smiled at him in a fierce and funny way. Tim smiled, too, and said, "Welcome back, Jack!"

To Nathaniel, Justin and especially Carol.

—W. H.

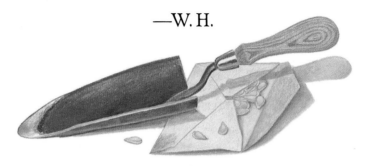

Library of Congress Cataloging-in-Publication Data
Hubbell, Will.
Pumpkin Jack / written and illustrated by Will Hubbell.
p. cm.

Summary: In the course of one year, a jack-o'-lantern, discarded after Halloween,
decomposes in the backyard and eventually grows new pumpkins from its seeds.
[1. Pumpkin — Fiction.  2. Jack-o'-lanterns — Fiction.  3. Halloween — Fiction.]  I. Title.
PZ7.H86312 Pu 2000  [E] — dc21   00-008282

Text and illustrations copyright © 2000 by Will Hubbell
Published in 2000 by Albert Whitman & Company
ISBN 978-0-8075-6666-4

Printed in China
18  17  16  15  14  13  NP  20  19  18  17  16  15

The illustrations are rendered in colored pencil with solvent wash effects.
The display typeface is Hornpype ITC. The text typeface is FC Artcraft Regular.
The design is by Will Hubbell and Scott Piehl.

For more information about Albert Whitman & Company,
visit our web site at www.albertwhitman.com.